D1028960

THE SEXTON
A SPECTATOR
HIS CONGREGATION
1
2
3
THE FARMER'S WIFE
THE BOY
THE OLD MAN
GREAT CLAUS

THE GRANDMOTHERS
TWO GOSSIPERS
THE APOTHECARY
THE FARMER
& THE INNKEEPER
LITTLE CLAUS

Great Claus and Little Claus

In a village there once
lived two men of the
NO

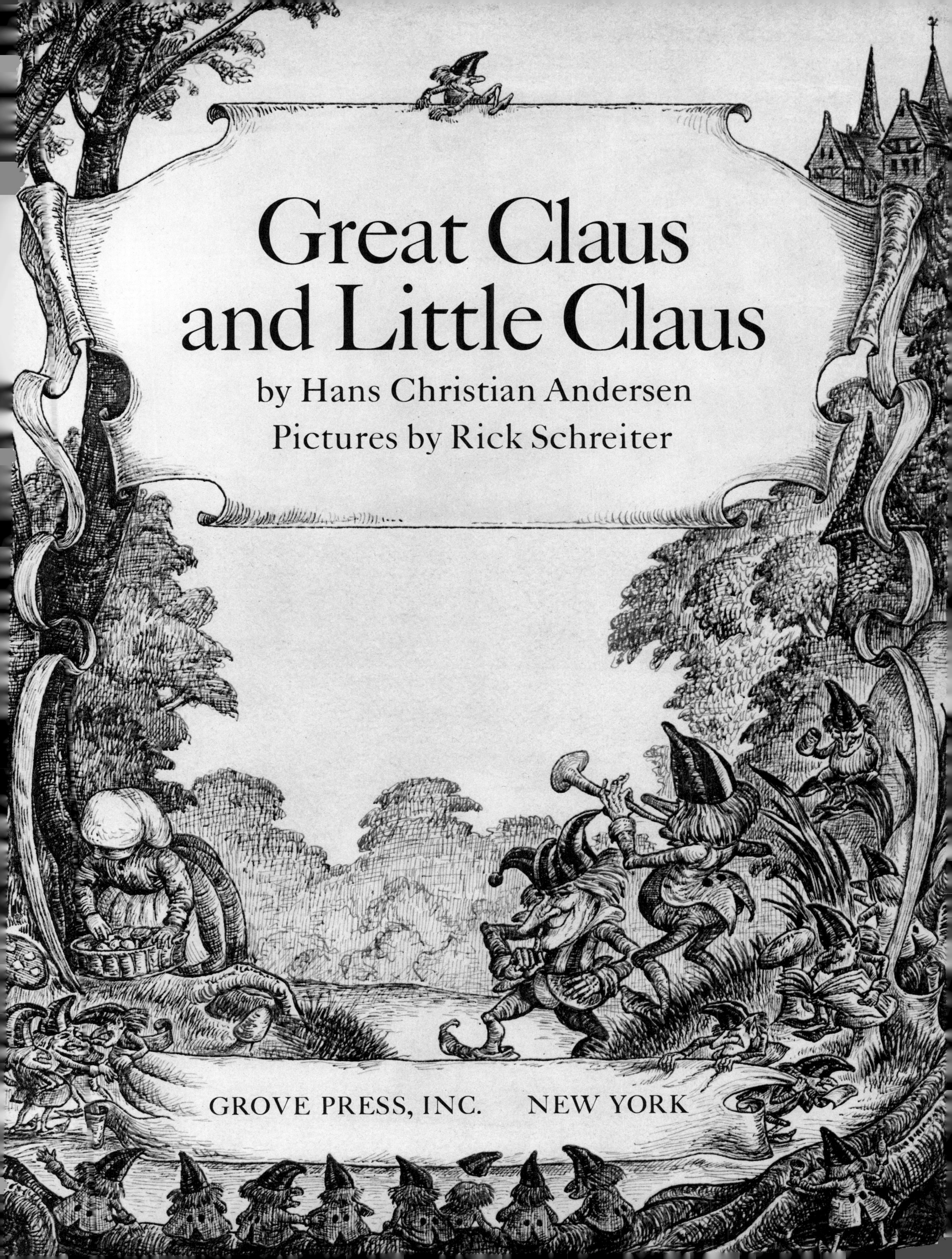

Great Claus and Little Claus

by Hans Christian Andersen

Pictures by Rick Schreiter

GROVE PRESS, INC. NEW YORK

Library of Congress Catalog Card Number: 68-8857
First Printing
Manufactured in the United States of America

n a village there once lived two men of the selfsame name. They were both called Claus, but one of them had four horses and the other had only one. So to distinguish them, people called the owner of the four horses "Great Claus," and he who had only one horse was called "Little Claus." Now I shall tell you what happened to them, for this is a true story.

Throughout the week Little Claus was obliged to plow for Great Claus and to lend him his one horse, but once a week—on Sunday—Great Claus lent him all his four horses. How proudly each Sunday Little Claus would smack his whip over all five, for they were as good as his own on that one day.

The sun shone brightly and the church bells rang merrily as the people passed by, dressed in their best and with their prayer books under their arms. They were going to hear the parson preach. They looked at Little Claus plowing with his five horses, and he was so proud that he smacked his whip and said, "Gee-up, my five horses."

"You mustn't say that," said Great Claus, "for only one of them is yours."

But Little Claus soon forgot what he ought not to say, and when anyone passed he would call out, "Gee-up, my five horses."

"I must really beg you not to say that again," said Great Claus. "If you do, I shall hit your horse on the head so that he will drop down dead on the spot. And that will be the end of him."

"I promise you I will not say it again," said the other. But as soon as anybody came by nodding to him and wishing him "Good day," he was so pleased and thought how grand it was to have five horses plowing in his field that he cried out again, "Gee-up, all my horses!"

"I'll gee-up your horses for you," said Great Claus. And seizing the tethering mallet he struck Little Claus's one horse on the head, and it fell down dead.

"Oh, now I have no horse at all," said Little Claus, weeping. But after a while he flayed the dead horse and hung the skin in the wind to dry.

Then he put the dried skin into a bag, hung it over his shoulder, and went off to the next town to sell it. But he had a long way to go and had to pass through a dark and gloomy forest.

Presently a storm arose and he lost his way. And before he discovered the right path, evening was drawing on, and it was still a long way to the town and too far to return home before nightfall.

Near the road stood a large farmhouse. The shutters outside the windows were closed, but lights shone through the crevices and at the top. "They might let me stay here for the night," thought Little Claus, so he went up to the door and knocked.

The farmer's wife opened the door, but when she heard what he wanted she told him to go away. Her husband was not at home and she could not let any strangers in.

"Then I shall have to lie out here," said Little Claus to himself, as the farmer's wife shut the door in his face.

Close to the farmhouse stood a large haystack, and between it and the house there was a small shed with a thatched roof. "I can lie up there," said Little Claus, as he saw the roof. "It will make a famous bed, but I hope the stork won't fly down and bite my legs." A live stork who had his nest on the roof was standing up there.

So Little Claus climbed on to the roof of the shed. And as he turned about to make himself comfortable, he discovered that the wooden shutters did not reach to the top of the windows. He could see into the room, in which a large table was

laid out with wine, roast meat, and a splendid fish. The farmer's wife and the sexton were sitting at table together. Nobody else was there. She was filling his glass and helping him plentifully to fish, which appeared to be his favorite dish.

"If only I could have some too," thought Little Claus. Then he stretched out his neck towards the window and spied a beautiful large cake. Indeed, they had a glorious feast before them.

At that moment he heard someone riding down the road towards the farm. It was the farmer coming home.

He was a good man but he had one very strange prejudice—he could not bear the sight of a sexton. If he happened to see one, he would get into a terrible rage. Because of this dislike, the sexton had gone to visit the farmer's wife during her husband's absence from home, and the good woman had put before him the best of everything she had in the house to eat.

When they heard the farmer they were dreadfully frightened, and the woman made the sexton creep into a large chest which stood in a corner. He went at once, for he was well aware of the poor man's aversion to the sight of a sexton. The woman then quickly hid all the nice things and the wine in the oven, because if her husband had seen it he would have asked why it was provided.

"Oh dear," sighed Little Claus, on the roof, when he saw the food disappearing.

"Is there anyone up there?" asked the farmer, peering up at Little Claus. "What are you doing up there? You had better come into the house."

Then Little Claus told him how he had lost his way, and asked if he might have shelter for the night.

"Certainly," said the farmer. "But the first thing is to have something to eat."

The woman received them both very kindly, laid the table, and gave them a large bowl of porridge. The farmer was hungry and ate it with a good appetite, but Little Claus could not help thinking of the good roast meat, the fish, and the cake, which he knew were hidden in the oven. He had put his sack with the hide in it under the table by his feet, for as we remember he was on his way to town to sell it. He did not fancy the porridge, so he trod on the sack and made the dried hide squeak quite loudly.

"Hush!" said Little Claus to his sack, at the same time treading on it again so that it squeaked louder than ever.

"What on earth have you got in your sack?" asked the farmer.

"Oh, it's a troll," said Little Claus. "He says we needn't eat the porridge, for he has charmed the oven full of roast meat and fish and cake."

"What do you say?" said the farmer, opening the oven door with all speed and seeing the nice things the woman had hidden, but which her husband thought the troll had produced for their special benefit.

The woman dared not say anything but put the food before them, and then they both made a hearty meal of the fish, the meat, and the cake.

Then Little Claus trod on the skin and made it squeak again.

"What does he say now?" asked the farmer.

"He says," answered Little Claus, "that he has also charmed three bottles of wine into the oven for us."

So the woman had to bring out the wine too, and the farmer drank it and became very merry. Wouldn't he like to have a troll for himself, like the one in Little Claus's sack!

"Can he charm out the devil?" asked the farmer. "I shouldn't mind seeing him, now that I am in such a merry mood."

"Oh yes!" said Little Claus. "My troll can do everything that we ask him. Can't you?" he asked, trampling on the sack till it squeaked louder than ever. "Did you hear him say yes? But the devil is so ugly, you'd better not see him."

"Oh, I'm not a bit frightened. Whatever does he look like?"

"Well, he will show himself in the image of a sexton."

"Oh dear!" said the farmer. "That's bad! I must tell you that I can't bear to see a sexton. However, it doesn't matter. I shall know it's only the devil and then I shan't mind so much. Now my courage is up! But he mustn't come too close."

"I'll ask my troll about it," said Little Claus, treading on the bag and putting his ear close to it.

"What does he say?"

"He says you can go along and open the chest in the corner, and there you'll see the devil moping in the dark. But hold the lid tight so that he doesn't get out."

"Will you help me to hold it?" asked the farmer, going along to the chest where the woman had hidden the real sexton, who was shivering with fright. The farmer lifted up the lid a wee little bit and peeped in.

"Ha!" he shrieked, and sprang back. "Yes, I saw him and he looked just exactly like our sexton. It was a horrible sight!" They had to have a drink after this, and there they sat drinking till far into the night.

"You must sell me that troll," said the farmer. "You may ask what you like for him! I'll give you a bushel of money for him."

"No, I can't do that," said Little Claus. "You must remember how useful my troll is to me."

"Oh, but I should so like to have him," said the farmer and he went on begging for him.

"Well," said Little Claus at last, "as you have been so kind to me I shall have to give him up. You shall have him for a bushel of money, but I must have it full to the brim."

"You shall have it," said the farmer. "But you must take that chest away with you! I won't have it in the house for another hour. I'd never know whether he's there or not."

So Little Claus gave his sack with the dried hide in it to the farmer and received in return a bushel of money, and the measure was full to the brim. The farmer also gave him a large wheelbarrow to take the money and the chest away in.

"Good-by," said Little Claus, and off he went with his money and the big chest with the sexton in it.

There was a wide and deep river on the other side of the wood. The current was so strong that it was almost impossible to swim against it. A large new bridge had been built across it, and when they got into the very middle of it, Little Claus said quite loud, so that the sexton could hear him, "What am I to do with this stupid old chest? It might be full of paving stones—it's so heavy. I am quite tired of wheeling it along, so I'll just throw it into the river. If it floats down the river to my house, well and good, and if it doesn't, I shan't care."

Then he took hold of the chest and raised it up a bit, as if he were about to throw it into the river.

"No, no! Let it be!" shouted the sexton. "Let me get out!"

"Hullo!" said Little Claus, pretending to be frightened. "Why, he's still inside it! Then I must heave it into the river to drown him."

"Oh no! Oh no!" shouted the sexton. "I'll give you a bushel full of money if you'll let me out!"

"Oh, that's another matter," said Little Claus, opening the chest. The sexton crept out at once and pushed the empty chest into the water, and then went home and gave Little Claus a whole bushel full of money. He had already had one from the farmer, you know, so now his wheelbarrow was quite full of money.

L. CLAUS

"I got a pretty fair price for that horse, I must admit," said he to himself when he got home to his own room and turned the money out of the wheelbarrow into a heap on the floor. "What a rage Great Claus will be in when he discovers how rich I have become through my one horse. But I won't tell him the truth about it."

So he sent a boy to Great Claus to borrow a bushel measure.

"What does he want that for?" thought Great Claus. And he rubbed some tallow on the bottom of the measure, so that a little of whatever was to be measured might stick to it. So it did, for when the measure came back three new silver threepenny bits were sticking to it.

"What's this?" said Great Claus, and he ran straight along to Little Claus. "Where on earth did you get all that money?"

"Oh, that was for my horse's hide which I sold last night."

"That was well paid indeed!" said Great Claus. And he ran home, took an ax, and hit all his four horses on the head. He then flayed them and went off to the town with the hides.

"Skins! Skins! Who will buy skins?" he shouted up and down the streets.

All the shoemakers and tanners in the town came running up and asked him how much he wanted for them.

"A bushel of money for each," said Great Claus.

"Are you mad?" they all said. "Do you imagine we have money by the bushel?"

"Skins! Skins! Who will buy skins?" he shouted again.

The shoemakers took up their measures and the tanners their leather aprons, and beat Great Claus through the town. "Skins! Skins!" they mocked him. "Yes, we'll give you a raw hide. Out of the town with him!" they shouted, and Great Claus had to hurry off as fast as ever he could go. He had never had such a beating in his life.

"Little Claus shall pay for this," he said when he got home. "I'll kill him for it."

PINCH·PAWNBROKER
LEATHER
BOOTS

Dr OF MEDICIN

Little Claus's old grandmother had just died in his house. She certainly had been very cross and unkind to him, but now that she was dead he felt quite sorry about it. He took the dead woman and put her into his warm bed to see if he could bring her to life again. He meant her to stay there all night, and he would sit on a chair in the corner. He had slept like that before.

As he sat there in the night, the door opened and in came Great Claus with his ax. He knew where Little Claus's bed stood, and he went straight up to it and hit the dead grandmother a blow on the forehead, thinking that it was Little Claus.

"Just see if you'll cheat me again after that," he said. Then he went home again.

"What a bad, wicked man he is," said Little Claus. "He was going to kill me there. What a good thing that poor old granny was dead already, or else he would have killed her."

He now dressed his old grandmother in her best Sunday clothes, borrowed a horse from his neighbor, harnessed it to a cart, and set his grandmother on the back seat so that she could not fall out when the cart moved. Then he started off through the woods. When the sun rose he was just outside a big inn, and Little Claus drew up his horse and went in to get something to eat. The landlord was a very, very rich man and a very good man, but he was fiery-tempered, as if he were made of pepper and tobacco.

"Good morning," said he to Little Claus. "You've got your best clothes on very early this morning!"

"Yes," said Little Claus. "I'm going to town with my old grandmother. She's sitting out there in the cart. I can't get her to come in. Won't you take her out a glass of mead? You'll have to shout at her, for she's very hard of hearing."

"Yes, she shall have it," said the innkeeper, and he poured out a large glass of mead which he took out to the dead grandmother in the cart.

"Here is a glass of mead your son has sent," said the innkeeper, but the dead woman sat quite still and never said a word. "Don't you hear?" shouted the innkeeper as loud as he could. "Here is a glass of mead from your son!"

Again he shouted and then again as loud as ever, but as she did not stir he got angry and threw the glass of mead in her face. The mead ran all over her and she fell backwards out of the cart, for she was only stuck up and not tied in.

"Now," shouted Little Claus, as he rushed out of the inn and seized the landlord by the neck. "You have killed my grandmother! Just look! There's a great hole in her forehead."

"Oh, what a misfortune!" exclaimed the innkeeper, clasping his hands. "That's the consequence of my fiery temper. Good Little Claus, I will give you a bushel of money and bury your grandmother as if she had been my own, if you will only say nothing about it. Otherwise they will chop my head off, and that is so nasty."

So Little Claus had a whole bushel of money, and the innkeeper buried the old grandmother just as if she had been his own.

When Little Claus got home again with all his money, he immediately sent his boy over to Great Claus to borrow his measure.

"What?" said Great Claus. "Is he not dead? I shall have to go and see about it myself." So he took the measure over to Little Claus himself.

"I say, wherever did you get all that money?" asked he, his eyes round with amazement at what he saw.

"It was my grandmother you killed instead of me," said Little Claus. "I have sold her and got a bushel of money for her."

"That was good pay indeed!" said Great Claus, so he hurried home, took an ax, and killed his old grandmother.

He then put her in a cart and drove off to town with her where the apothecary lived, and asked if he would buy a dead body.

"Who is it, and where did the body come from?" asked the apothecary.

"It is my grandmother, and I have killed her for a bushel of money," said Great Claus.

"Heaven preserve us!" said the apothecary. "You are talking like a madman. Pray don't say such things! You might lose your head." And he pointed out to him what a horribly wicked thing he had done and what a bad man he was, and that he deserved to be punished. Great Claus was so frightened that he rushed straight out of the shop, jumped into the cart, whipped up his horse, and galloped

THOMAS TOLL · APOTHECARY

home. The apothecary and everyone else thought he was mad, and so they let him drive off.

"You shall be paid for this!" said Great Claus, when he got out on the high-road. "You shall pay for this, Little Claus!"

As soon as he got home, he took the biggest sack he could find, went over to Little Claus and said, "You have deceived me again. First I killed my horses, and then my old grandmother. It's all your fault, but you shan't have the chance of cheating me again!" Then he took Little Claus by the waist and put him into the sack, put it on his back, and shouted to him, "I'm going to drown you now!"

It was a long way to go before he came to the river, and Little Claus was not so light to carry. The road passed close by a church in which the organ was playing, and the people were singing beautifully. Great Claus put down the sack with Little Claus in it close by the church door. He thought he would like to go and hear a psalm before he went any further. As Little Claus could not get out of the bag, and all the people were in the church, Great Claus went in too.

"Oh dear, oh dear!" sighed Little Claus in the sack. He turned and twisted, but it was impossible to undo the cord. Just then an old cattle drover with white hair and a tall stick in his hand came along. He had a whole drove of cows and bulls before him. They ran against the sack Little Claus was in and upset it.

"Oh dear," sighed Little Claus. "I am so young to be going to the Kingdom of Heaven!"

"And I," said the cattle drover, "am so old and cannot get there yet!"

"Open the sack!" shouted Little Claus. "Get inside in place of me, and you will get to Heaven directly."

"That will just suit me," said the cattle drover, undoing the sack for Little Claus, who immediately sprang out. "You must look after the cattle now," said the old man as he crept into the sack. Little Claus tied it up and walked off driving the cattle before him.

YE CHOIRMASTER
HO HUM
3

BLESS YE ALL

A little while afterwards Great Claus came out of the church. He took the sack again on his back and he certainly thought it had grown lighter, for the old cattle drover was not more than half the weight of Little Claus.

"How light he seems to have got! That must be because I have been to church and said my prayers." Then he went on to the river, which was both wide and deep, and threw the sack with the old cattle drover in it into the water.

"Now, you won't cheat me again!" he shouted, for he thought it was Little Claus.

Then he went homewards, but when he reached the crossroads he met Little Claus with his herd of cattle.

"What's the meaning of this?" exclaimed Great Claus. "Didn't I drown you?"

"Yes," said Little Claus. "It's just about half an hour since you threw me into the river."

"But where did you get all those splendid beasts?" asked Great Claus.

"They are sea cattle," said Little Claus. "I will tell you the whole story, and indeed I thank you heartily for drowning me. I'm at the top of the tree now and a very rich man, I can tell you. I was so frightened when I was in the sack! The wind whistled in my ears when you threw me over the bridge into the cold water. I immediately sank to the bottom but I was not hurt, for the grass is beautifully soft down there. The sack was opened at once by a beautiful maiden in snow-white clothes with a green wreath on her wet hair. She took my hand and said, 'Are you there, Little Claus? Here are some cattle for you, and a mile further up the road you will come upon another herd which I will give you too!' Then I saw that the river was a great highway for the sea folk. Down at the bottom of it they walked and drove about, from the sea right up to the end of the river. The flowers were lovely and the grass was so fresh! The fishes which swam about glided close to me just like birds in the air. How nice the people were, and what a lot of cattle strolled about in the ditches!"

"But why did you come straight up here again then?" asked Great Claus. "I shouldn't have done that if it was so fine down there."

TO THE RIVE
TO TOWN 1Km

"Oh," said Little Claus, "that's just my cunning. You remember I told you the mermaid said that a mile further up the road—and by the road she means the river, for she can't go anywhere else—I should find another herd of cattle waiting for me. Well, I know how many bends there are in the river and what a roundabout way it would be. It's ever so much shorter if you can come up on dry land and take the short cuts. You save a couple of miles by it and can get the cattle much sooner."

"Oh, you *are* a fortunate man," said Great Claus. "Do you think I should get some sea cattle if I were to go down to the bottom of the river?"

"I'm sure you would," said Little Claus. "But I can't carry you in the sack to the river. You're too heavy for me. If you'd like to walk there and then get into the sack, I'll throw you into the river with the greatest pleasure in the world."

"Thank you," said Great Claus. "But if I don't get any sea cattle when I get down there, see if I don't give you a sound thrashing."

"Oh, don't be so hard on me!" said Little Claus.

Then they walked off to the river. As soon as the cattle saw the water they rushed down to drink, for they were very thirsty. "See what a hurry they're in," said Little Claus. "They want to get down to the bottom again."

"Now, help me first," said Great Claus, "or else I'll thrash you." He then crept into a big sack which had been lying across the back of one of the cows. "Put a big stone in, or I'm afraid I shan't sink," said Great Claus.

"Oh, have no fear of that," said Little Claus, and he put a big stone into the sack and gave it a push. Plump went the sack and Great Claus was in the river, where he sank to the bottom at once.

"I'm afraid he won't find any cattle," said Little Claus, as he drove his herd home.

I believe—and it will please me if I am right—that I have realized the art of writing fairy-tales. The first I turned out were mostly the older ones I had heard as a child, and which I, according to my nature and style, gladly told and reworked; those I created myself, however, won the greatest applause, and this has given me wings. Now I speak from my own breast, seize on an idea for the elders and tell it for the little ones, keeping in mind that father and mother are listening in, and they deserve a little to think about. I have a mass of material, more than for any other literary form; for me it is often as though every hoarding, every little flower was saying: "You have but to look at me and my story will unfold within you," and if I do, I have the story.

—Hans Christian Andersen
from a letter to a friend, 1843